Take Our Dog to the Veterinarian

1. Get a New Pet Health Check
2. He has to get shots. ☹
3. He needs yearly check-ups

a dog is shy-

sk, "May I pet the dog?"

If she says, "Yes."
old your hand out, ingers down.

alk softly.

Let him sniff your fingers.

If he's wagging his tail, he wants to be petted.

If he stiffens up, he's saying, "No, thank you!"

Dogs aren't the only animals we can find in an animal shelter. They also have cats, rabbits, turtles, birds, and even horses!

is:

r

ewer

ne

We Really, Really Want a Dog!

By Susan Holt Kralovansky

PELICAN PUBLISHING
New Orleans 2021

ISBN: 9781455625871
Ebook ISBN: 9781455625888

Printed in Korea
Published by Pelican Publishing
New Orleans, LA
www.pelicanpub.com

For Jake, Sunny, Seth, and Layla, and for shelter dogs everywhere
With gratitude to Robert Crane for the photography

We want a dog!
We really, really want a dog!

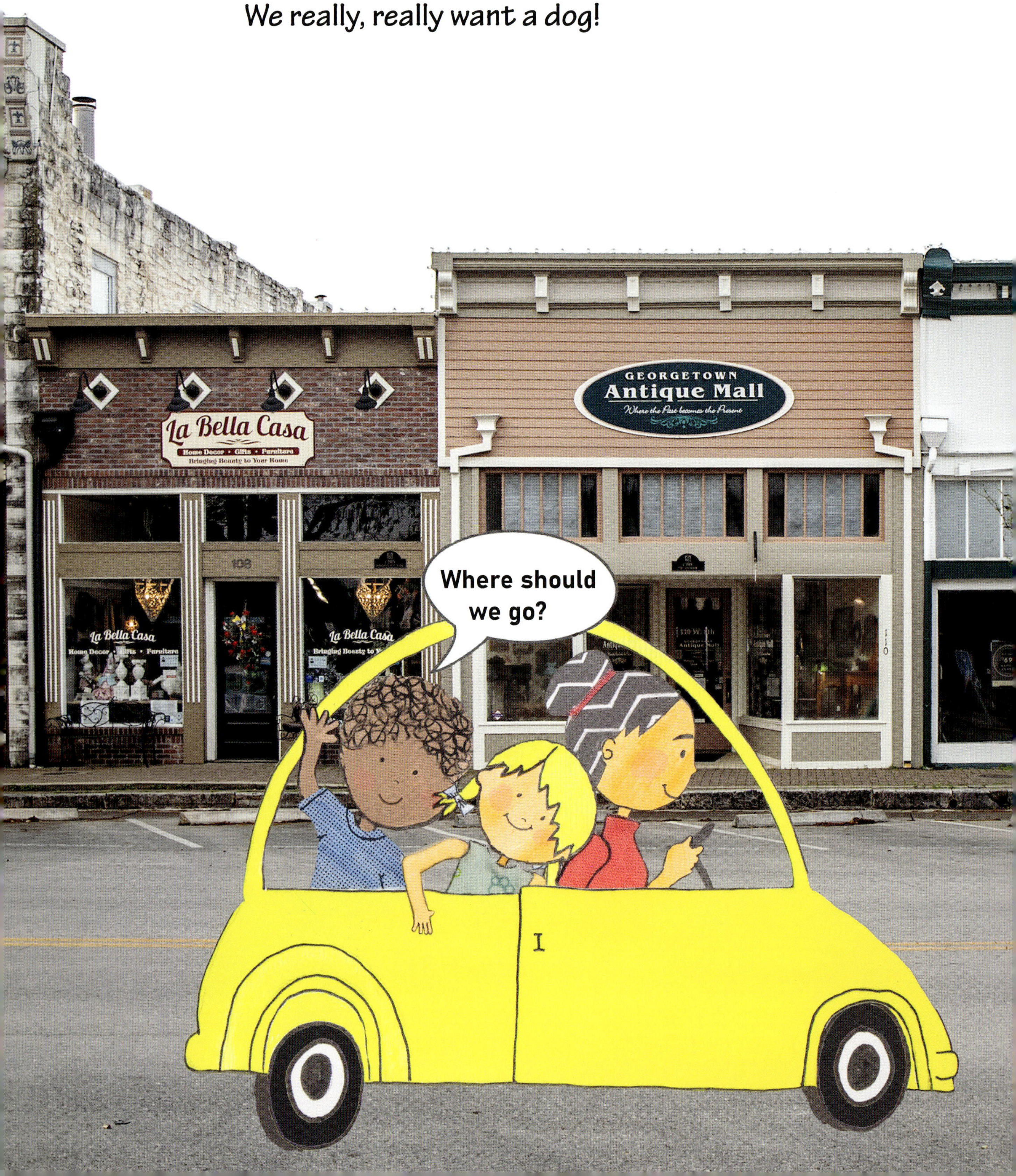

An animal shelter is a perfect place to look.
When you adopt a dog, you save its life!

At the shelter,
you will see . . .
tall dogs
and small dogs,

old dogs
and puppies,
purebreds
and mixed breeds.
So many wonderful dogs all
waiting for a home.

But your mother says you can only have one.

"One?" you say.

"One?" your sister says. "How can we choose only one?"

You moan. She groans.

But your mom doesn't budge.

"Okay," you sigh. "Just one."

"But, which one?" your sister asks.

Take along a notebook and ask questions.

Does this one play fetch?

Does he shed?

Does this one like cats?

Does she know any tricks?

How big will that puppy get?

Does this one like other dogs?

Does he like kids?

There are all types of dogs at an animal shelter waiting to be loved.

“How about that one?” you say.
“He’s not too big,” your sister says.
“He’s not too small,” you say.
“He’s just right!” you both say.
Finally, you’ve found your perfect pooch!

First you had questions. Now the shelter staff has questions for you. But don't worry, you've both done your research.

"Do you really, *really* want a dog?"

"Yes!"

"Will you take him outside often to go to the bathroom?"

"Yes! If we don't, he might have accidents . . .

on the carpet,

or under my bed,

or behind the washing machine!"

"Will you feed your dog every day? And give him fresh water?"

"Yes! If we don't, he might . . .

get in the garbage,

or grab food off the table,

or drink out of the toilet! Yuck!"

"Will you walk your dog every day?"
"Yes! If we don't, our dog might . . .

gain too much weight,

or bark,

or chew everything!"

"Will you play with your dog?"
"*Yes!* Because we all need . . .

to run,

and play catch,

and learn tricks."

Make an appointment with a veterinarian, a doctor who treats animals. The vet will tell you what to do to keep your dog healthy.

And finally, the shelter staff will say, "If you're *going* to feed, water, and play with your pet, I think you really, really, *really do* want a dog."

You have a new forever friend! You'll want to take it slow. Give him a few days to get used to . . .

your family,

and your house,

and your backyard.

When he's comfortable, you can take him on adventures . . .
through your neighborhood,
and to meet your friends,
and to see the dog next door.

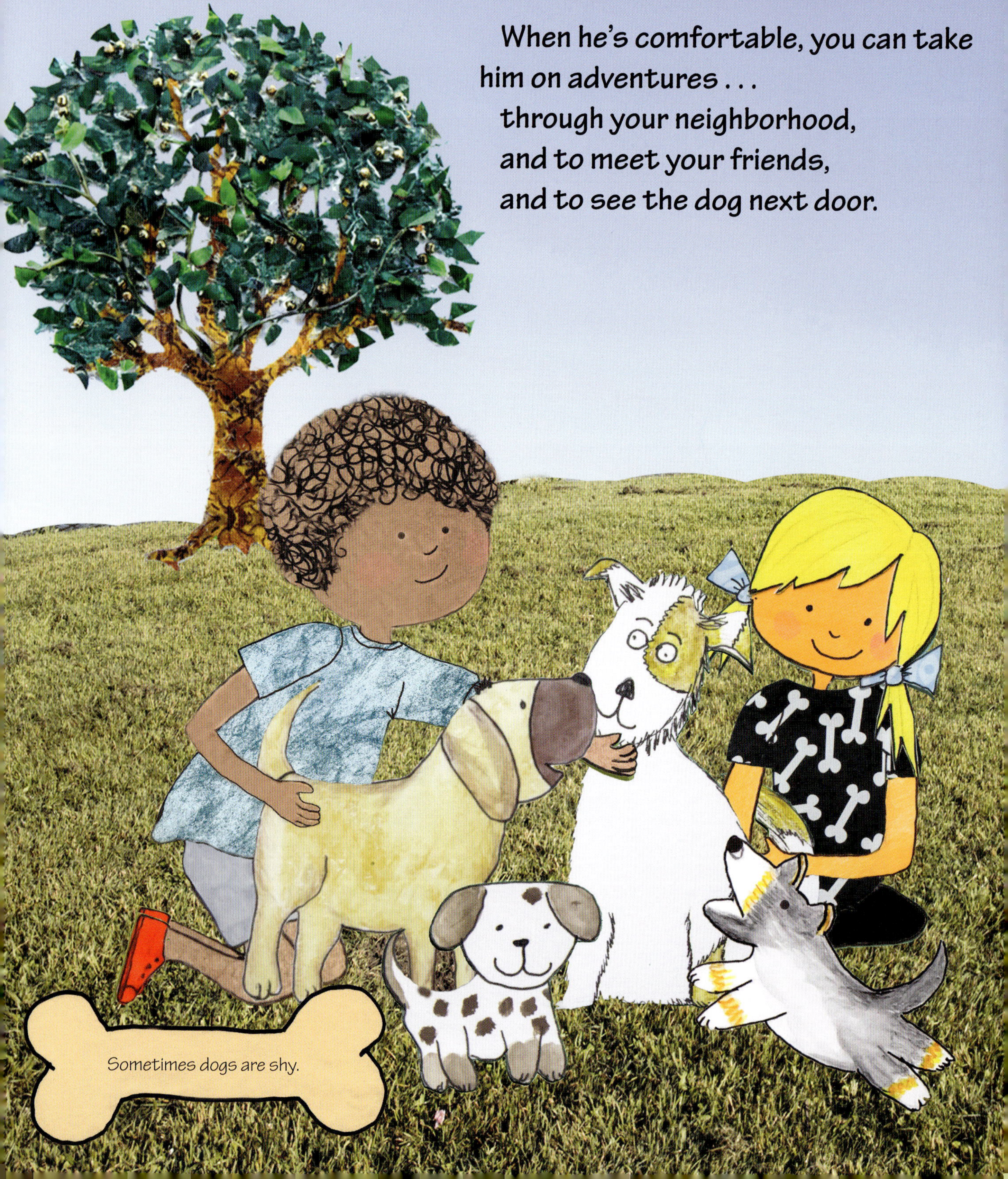

Sometimes dogs are shy.

After you've taken a walk, or gone to the park, or played ball, your new friend might need . . .
some food,
and water.

And when he starts to explore, he probably has to go to the bathroom.

When he's done, you'll probably all need a nap. You can fix up a little spot for him . . .

in a crate, or in the corner,

or maybe on the bed, sharing your blanket and pillow.

He might like to sit with his head on your knee,
and his paw in your sister's hand,
and you'll all sigh.

Then . . .
as you're scratching his ear,
and looking into his big doggy eyes,
you'll realize . . .
he's going to be lonely when you're at school.

And you'll yell,

"Mom! We have to go back to the shelter!
Our dog wants a cat!
He really, really, *really* wants a cat!"

Author's Note

Ready for a pet?

Adopt your next cat or dog from a shelter or other rescue organization. Two of the most famous are the Humane Society of the United States and the American Society for the Prevention of Cruelty to Animals (ASPCA). Your city and county may have other shelters as well. Shelters give pets a new life with owners like you, as well as spaying or neutering them so they won't mate. They will also let you "try out" a pet to see if it is a good fit for both you and the animal.

A shelter's goal is to:

- find responsible people to adopt pets;
- help people understand that shelter animals make fantastic family pets;
- and raise awareness about the importance of spaying and neutering for population control.

Most shelters will:

- do their best to provide healthy, adoptable animals;
- provide pre-adoption tests and veterinary care;
- evaluate each animal's temperament;
- and give you as much information as possible about the animal's behavior and personality.

Online Resources:

The Humane Society of the United States is the nation's largest and most effective animal protection organization.
www.humanesociety.org

American Society for the Prevention of Cruelty to Animals (ASPCA) was the first humane society to be established in North America.
www.aspca.org/

National Geographic for Kids, Pet Central has photography tips, videos, pet care guides, stories of amazing pets, and pet games.
kids.nationalgeographic.com/explore/pet-central/

PBS Kids for dog games.
pbskids.org/games/dog/

Making a Toy for Your Furry Friend

Don't toss those old socks. Cut them up and make the perfect crackle dog toy.

Supplies:

1. Cut the toe off of a sock.

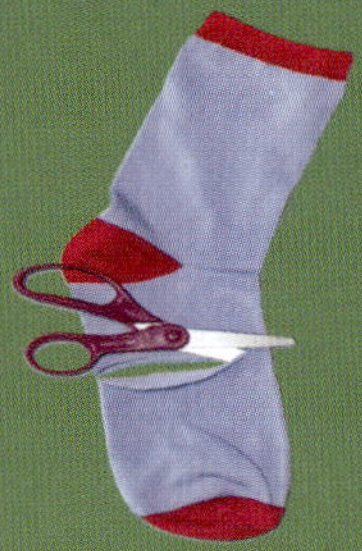

2. Slide the bottle into the sock.

3. Cut two pieces of ribbon, 10 inches each.

4. Use the ribbon to tie the top and the bottom of the sock closed.

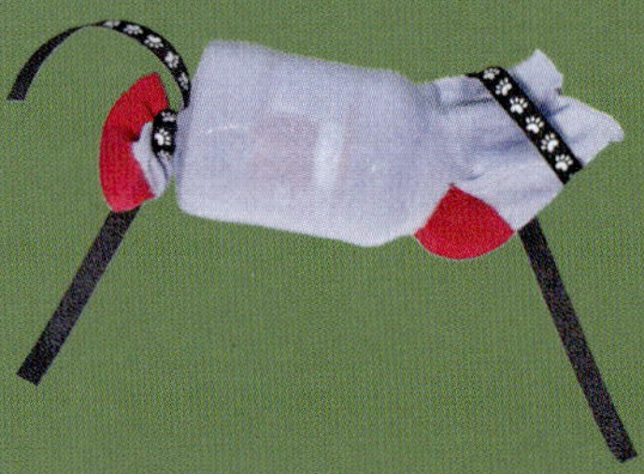

You can make extra toys and donate them to a shelter.

5. Let your dog play with his new Crackly Toy.

A special thank you to the Texas Humane Heroes for providing dog photographs. These dogs have been adopted, but there are many more that need a home.